Boris Goes Camping

For my Mum and Dad x. – C.W.

For Toby 'Toto' Ridgway. – T.W.

Also available
Boris Starts School

OXFORD
UNIVERSITY PRESS

Great Clarendon Street, Oxford OX2 6DP

Oxford University Press is a department of the University of Oxford.
It furthers the University's objective of excellence in research, scholarship,
and education by publishing worldwide in

Oxford New York

Auckland Cape Town Dar es Salaam Hong Kong Karachi
Kuala Lumpur Madrid Melbourne Mexico City Nairobi
New Delhi Shanghai Taipei Toronto

With offices in
Argentina Austria Brazil Chile Czech Republic France Greece
Guatemala Hungary Italy Japan Poland Portugal Singapore
South Korea Switzerland Thailand Turkey Ukraine Vietnam

British Library Cataloguing in Publication Data available

ISBN: 978-0-19-278979-2 (paperback)

10 9 8 7 6 5 4 3 2 1

Printed in China

Paper used in the production of this book is a natural, recyclable product made
from wood grown in sustainable forests. The manufacturing process conforms
to the environmental regulations of the country of origin

Carrie Weston • Tim Warnes

Boris Goes Camping

OXFORD
UNIVERSITY PRESS

The day that Miss Cluck was taking the class camping, everyone was very excited.

When Miss Cluck said that it was almost time to set off, all the animals squealed with delight.

Leticia the rabbit
carried her butterfly net.

Leticia

Maxwell the mole
clutched his Teddy.

The little mice
each had a basket.

Fergus the fox cub
was given the map.

And Boris was put in charge of . . .

absolutely everything else!
For Boris was an enormous,
hairy, scary, grizzly bear . . .
but he was also rather kind and helpful.

'Bravo!'
said Miss Cluck
as Boris heaved the
huge bag on his back.
'What would we
do without you?'

'Phew!'

Miss Cluck and her class set off through the woods.

'Whee!'

Leticia chased after butterflies.

Fergus puzzled over the map.

Maxwell got Teddy stuck up a tree.

And the mice struggled with their baskets.

Eventually Boris caught up with them all.

Poor Miss Cluck
blew her whistle.
'This really won't do,'
she said, 'we must
stay together.'

'But we're tired!'

Then Boris had an idea.

He found room for everything in his bag. Even the tired mice.

'Bravo, Boris!' cheered his friends.

Before long they came to a little bridge.

Boris and Leticia dropped twigs into the stream.

'Come on, Boris!'

'Go, Leticia!'

Then everyone rushed to the other side of the bridge to see whose would come out first.

But somehow, Boris forgot about the bag on his back.

Somehow, Maxwell's Teddy went **splash!** into the water.

Somehow, the mice managed to cling on.

Maxwell let out an enormous wail.
'**Oh, Boris!**' he cried.

Poor Boris felt so clumsy and ashamed.

Miss Cluck carefully leaned
over the bridge with Leticia's
butterfly net, but it was no good.
Teddy
was
floating
away.

Boris decided it
was time to be
very brave.
He leapt into
the water . . .

splash!

all the way
up to his
hairy knees!

Boris scooped Teddy safely out of the water.
Now there were two dripping-wet bears.

And Maxwell
hugged
them both.

'Boris is the biggest, bravest, best bear!' said Maxwell.

'Bravo, Boris!'

'Bravo, Boris!' agreed Miss Cluck. 'Now let's set up camp before there are any more accidents.'

The animals gathered around while Miss Cluck explained how to build a tepee. It all sounded very easy.

Leticia and Maxwell collected long sticks.

The mice chewed off some lengths of rope.

'Nibble!' 'Nibble!'

Boris helped Fergus spread out the canvas.

Then they all tried to put it together.

But it was not easy . . . not at all easy.

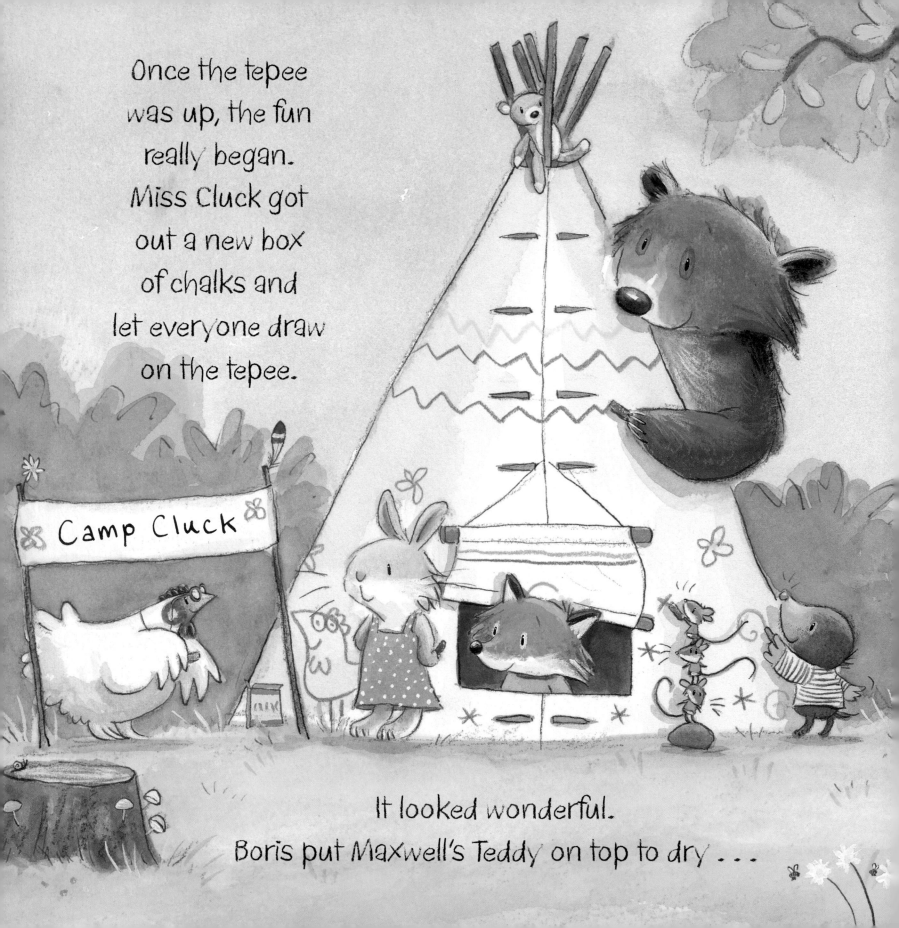

Once the tepee was up, the fun really began. Miss Cluck got out a new box of chalks and let everyone draw on the tepee.

Camp Cluck

It looked wonderful.
Boris put Maxwell's Teddy on top to dry . . .

and off they went to pick berries for supper. Miss Cluck showed them which ones were good to eat.

Boris carried the full baskets while the other animals hurried excitedly back to camp.

But they were in for a shock!

For their wonderful tepee wasn't
quite so wonderful any more.
Someone had drawn on Miss Cluck's face.
Someone had pulled down all the sticks . . .

and someone was going to be in **BIG** trouble!

Miss Cluck was very, very angry indeed. She marched straight up to the bulging canvas, reached underneath, and pulled out . . .

two very naughty little wolf cubs.
The cubs wriggled and struggled.

'Do your parents know you are out in the woods alone?' asked Miss Cluck in her firmest voice.

'We don't care!' yelled one of the cubs rudely.
'Our daddy is a **big,**
bad
wolf!'

'He's much **bigger** than you,' said the other,
even more rudely, 'and he **eats chickens** for . . .'

The naughty little wolf cubs
turned on their heels and fled.
Boris was most confused.

'Aaaaagghhh!'

'Oh, Boris, what a brave bear you are,'
smiled Miss Cluck,
'now let's
put the tepee
back together.'

'Bravo
for hairy,
scary Boris!'

That evening Boris and his friends ate a supper of toasted marshmallows and berries until the sun went down.

Then Miss Cluck got out her guitar and they sang songs under the stars.

'Kum Bay Ya!'

Boris felt his eyelids grow heavy.
It was tiring being a big, brave bear.
'I think I might go to bed now,' he yawned.

'Sleep tight!'

'Good night, Boris.'

'Night night!'

Boris snuggled down
happily inside the tepee
and was soon snoring.

A little later, Fergus, then Leticia, Maxwell with Teddy, the mice, and Miss Cluck crept into the tepee.

There wasn't much room but nobody minded a bit. After all, everyone had a nice, soft place to sleep . . .

even Miss Cluck.

'Bravo, Boris,' she whispered
as she fell asleep.